W9-DBR-096

TOM'S TAIL

By Arlene Dubanevich

B O M V O

This belongs to

PUFFIN BOOKS

PUFFIN BOOKS
Published by the Penguin Group
Penguin Books USA Inc., 375 Hudson Street, New York, New York 10014, U.S.A.
Penguin Books Ltd, 27 Wrights Lane, London W8 5TZ, England
Penguin Books Australia Ltd, Ringwood, Victoria, Australia
Penguin Books Canada Ltd, 10 Alcorn Avenue, Toronto, Ontario, Canada M4V 3B2
Penguin Books (N.Z.) Ltd, 182–190 Wairau Road, Auckland 10, New Zealand

Penguin Books Ltd, Registered Offices: Harmondsworth, Middlesex, England

First published in the United States of America by Viking Penguin,
a division of Penguin Books USA Inc., 1990
Published in Puffin Books, 1992

1 3 5 7 9 10 8 6 4 2

Copyright © Arlene Dubanevich, 1990
All rights reserved

LIBRARY OF CONGRESS CATALOGING-IN-PUBLICATION DATA
Dubanevich, Arlene.
    Tom's tail / by Arlene Dubanevich.   p. cm.
    Summary: An old tomcat grows increasingly lazy and sleepy, despite
the presence of many mischievous mice.
    ISBN 0-14-054177-2
    [1. Cats—Fiction. 2. Mice—Fiction. 3. Stories in rhyme.] I. Title.
    [PZ8.3.D85To 1992]   [E]—dc20   92-8615

Printed in the United States of America
Set in Rockwell Light

Except in the United States of America, this book is sold subject
to the condition that it shall not, by way of trade or otherwise,
be lent, re-sold, hired-out, or otherwise circulated without the
publisher's prior consent in any form of binding or cover other than
that in which it is published and without a similar condition including
this condition being imposed on the subsequent purchaser.

To Dad —AD

Old Tom was slipping,
losing his touch.
Old Tom was sleeping,
sleeping too much.

His days were a haze
of catnaps and catnips.
Tom barely could manage
short outside trips.

When mice were about
Tom used to jump.
Now he just lay there,
a lump in a slump.

In spring Tom hissed
at the thought of a mouse....
By fall things were mousy
all over the house.

Mice who should quietly
tiptoe and sneak,
gleefully gathered
to laugh, lunch, and squeak.

Those beady-eyed beasties
played in plain sight.
Played all day.
Played all night.

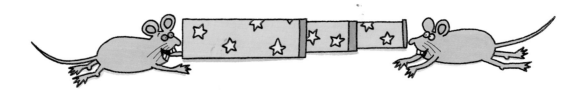

Old Tom was slipping,
losing his touch.
Tom had turned lazy.
He wasn't worth much.

Tom was out cold,
so he didn't hear
tiny mouse voices
right next to his ear.

Soon others joined in
with those first little pests,
but nothing they said
could rouse Tom from his rest.

Mice pulled his whiskers.
They tickled his toes.
They couldn't believe
Tom continued to doze.

Just as a joke
old Tom was poked.
He was warm and breathing
but he never awoke.

One mouse took command.
He said, "FOLLOW MY TRAIL."
Mice marched to the rear
and tugged on Tom's tail.

The tail that was Tom's
started to bend.
Those mice were caught holding
the end of the end.

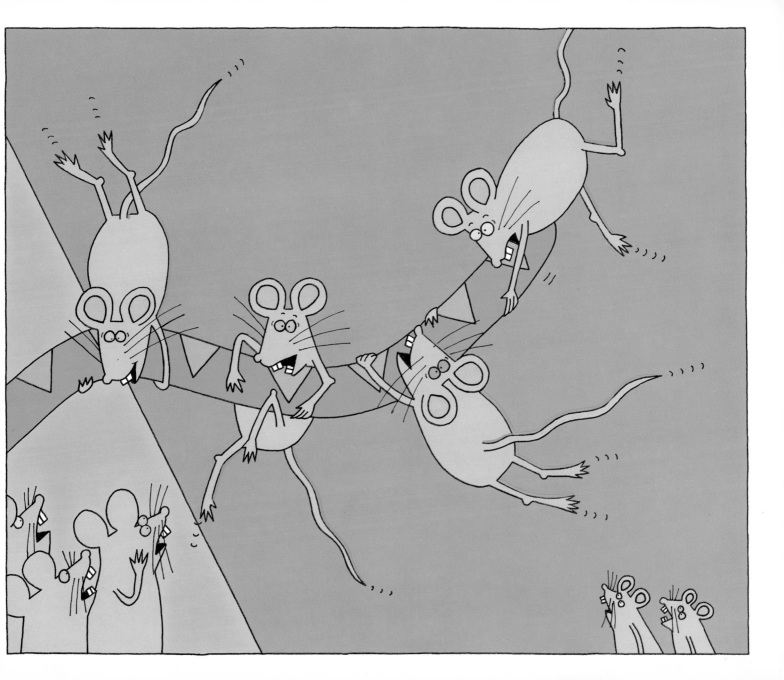

Mousies aren't known
for thinking ahead.
"WE DIDN'T MEAN IT!"
they screamed as they fled.

Now when Tom sleeps,
he keeps order and law
with one eye open ...
and his tail 'neath his paw.